KT-394-385

Contents

Get that Ghost to Go!

by

Catherine MacPhail

Illustrated by Karen Donnelly

You do not need to read this page –
just get on with the book!

J186.914   €9.00

First published in 2003 in Great Britain by
Barrington Stoke Ltd, Sandeman House, Trunk's Close,
55 High Street, Edinburgh EH1 1SR
www.barringtonstoke.co.uk

Reprinted 2005

ISBN 1-842991-31-0

Printed in Great Britain by Bell & Bain Ltd

MEET THE AUTHOR – CATHERINE MACPHAIL

What is your favourite animal?
Elephant
What is your favourite boy's name?
David
What is your favourite girl's name?
Sarah
What is your favourite food?
Prawns
What is your favourite music?
Dean Martin singing
That's Amore
What is your favourite hobby?
Writing

MEET THE ILLUSTRATOR – KAREN DONNELLY

What is your favourite animal?
Woodlice!
What is your favourite boy's name?
Laurie
What is your favourite girl's name?
Jean
What is your favourite food?
Sausages and runny eggs
What is your favourite music?
Beck
What is your favourite hobby?
Drawing and printmaking

To the Spateson Boys —
Mark, Greg, Duncan, Dean and Ross

Chapter 1
Markie and Me

It all started one day after school when Markie and me were playing football in the park.

Well, Markie was playing football. I was in goal, leaning against the posts, watching Markie dribbling the ball. He was showing off to the girls who were standing at the side and cheering him on.

Girls always watch Markie. He's the best looking boy in the school. I know, because he told me. I'm Duncan, by the way, and Markie's my best pal. Him and I are what you call "cool". We dress cool. We act cool. We are cool.

We weren't in the football team. We weren't in a gang. Lots of people would have liked to be our friends, but Markie and me didn't need anybody else. There were some people in the school who didn't even like us! They thought we were a couple of show-offs. We weren't show-offs. We were just better than everybody else.

Anyway, Markie was bouncing the ball off his head when I heard barking and yelping from across the park. I looked over and there was Ross, trying to control a bunch of his dogs on leads. They were pulling away from him as if they were scared. Terrified, in fact. They were jumping

and whining, and Ross kept tripping over
as he tried to hold them back.

Ross came from this strange family who were always taking in stray dogs. I had lost count of just how many they had. I would hate to see the mess their house is in.

Ross looked like a stray himself. He wore long woollen jumpers, all different colours and his dark hair was always standing on end like a toilet brush.

Ross would have liked to be our friend too. He waved at us every day when he came to the park. But Ross? A friend of ours? Come on. Get real.

What was wrong with those dogs? Every day, as soon as they came into the park, it was as if they were really scared of something. I knew what would happen next. They'd suddenly leap away with Ross in tow, and he would be dragged around the park on his belly.

It was great fun to watch.

I was so busy looking over at Ross that I didn't notice that Markie had stopped bouncing the ball on his head and had sent it flying towards the goal. It was only at the last moment that I turned and saw the ball racing at me like a comet about to crash into Earth.

"Duncan!" Markie yelled at me, but it was too late. The ball slammed into my face and everything went black.

When I came to, Markie was bending over me. In fact, there seemed to be two Markies. "Are you all right?" they both said. "Duncan, pal, speak to me!"

I blinked and tried to focus.

Suddenly, the girls came rushing up to us. "Did you hurt yourself?" They sounded really worried.

I was just about to answer when I realised that they weren't talking to me. They were talking to Markie.

"I'm the one who was knocked out!" I told them as Markie helped me to my feet. They weren't interested. Not in me. They gathered round Markie like a fan club and led him off to make sure he hadn't hurt his foot when he kicked the ball.

I rubbed my eyes and tried to see things more clearly. I could still hear those dogs howling. I blinked a few more times and looked over at them.

No wonder they were howling. Some tall, lanky boy with red hair was kicking them. That made me mad. I hate to see animals getting hurt. I ran across to him. "You leave those dogs alone!" I yelled.

Ross looked up at me. "Me? I've not touched them."

"Not you. *Him*!" I pointed at the red-haired boy. I noticed now that he was dressed funny. He wore a long black jacket and tight black trousers that looked like drainpipes. His black shoes had long pointed toes. Wow! I wouldn't like to be kicked by them. His hair too was swept up in a wave you could have surfed on.

He looked totally surprised. "Can you see me?"

"Of course I can see you. If you kick those dogs one more time, you'll be sorry."

Ross looked at me as if he was ready to cry. "Me? I'd never kick my dogs."

"Not you, Ross. *Him*!"

I pointed again at the red-haired boy who stuck out his tongue at me. "Make me stop!" he said and he aimed another kick at the dogs.

That was it! I flung myself at the boy.

And that's when the most amazing thing happened.

I went right through him.

The dogs went bounding away across the park dragging Ross behind them.

I landed on the grass and yelled at the top of my voice, "What happened?"

The red-haired boy was dancing about like a wild man. "Brilliant!" he shouted. "You can see me. Nobody's ever been able to see me before."

"See you?" I said. "What do you mean?" I was beginning to think I was still knocked out.

"Are you thick?" He leaned down to me. He smelled awful. And I saw now that he had one blue eye and one green eye. I was beginning to have a really bad feeling about what was going on.

"I'm a ghost," he said softly.

Chapter 2
Spooked

I think I fainted again. When I opened my eyes Markie was slapping my face.

"Are you OK, pal?" he said.

"I had an awful dream, Markie," I said. I began to tell him, but I couldn't get the words out. Right in front of me was the tall boy with the red hair, black jacket and pointed shoes. He was standing near Markie, grinning in a very nasty way.

"Can you see him, Markie?" I pointed my finger at the boy, so close I was nearly touching his face.

Markie looked round. "Who? Do you mean Ross?" He began to laugh, because there in the distance was Ross, still being dragged around on his belly behind his dogs.

"Not Ross, no – *him*!"

Markie followed my pointing finger closely till he was staring right into the red-haired boy's face, only inches away from him. The boy stuck out his tongue. I waited for Markie to punch him. The boy wouldn't get away with that.

Instead, Markie turned back to me and said, "Nobody there, pal." Then he sniffed. "But there's one awful smell. Was that you?"

The boy started jumping like a Mexican jumping bean. "Nobody else can see me! Nobody else can see me!" He was whooping with joy. "This is going to be great. I've never haunted a person before."

I grabbed at Markie's shirt. "You've got to be able to see that boy," I said. "If you can't, it means he really is a ..."

But he couldn't be a ... *ghost*. He was as solid as me and Markie. He looked just the same as everybody else, except for a green glow all around him – and that smell.

"He's a what?" Markie asked.

I took a deep breath. I could hardly say it, "He's a ghost."

"I am a ghost!" the boy yelled. "And my name's Dean, by the way. If I'm going to haunt you we might as well be friends."

"He says his name's Dean. And he's going to haunt me."

Markie looked worried. "It was that bump on the head. That's why you're seeing things. I'm going to take you home."

"I'm coming too," Dean said.

"NO!" I screamed it out and Markie looked hurt.

"I'm only trying to help you, Duncan."

"I'm not talking to you!" I shouted at Markie. "I'm talking to him."

If there is one thing about Markie, it's this. He's the best friend you could ever have. I know, because he told me. At that moment he proved he was my best friend.

"If you say there's a ghost there, I'm going to believe you. You would never lie to me." Markie stood up. "Right. Where is he? I'm going to sort him out."

He pushed up his sleeves ready for a fight. And let me tell you, Markie is the best fighter in the school. I know, because he told me. Not that I've known him to fight with anybody. He usually gets them laughing first.

Markie held up his fists and started darting about the way boxers do. "Now, tell me where this ghost is. I'm going to punch him."

Poor Markie didn't stand a chance. I watched in horror as Dean drew in his breath and let it out in one gigantic blow. It was like a whirlwind. Markie was lifted from his feet and thrown across the park.

I jumped to my feet. "You're evil," I yelled.

Dean made a stupid face. "I'm a ghost. You expect me to be nice?"

I ran over to Markie. He was lying in a bush, covered in mud.

"Was that the ghost?" he asked, spitting out dead leaves.

"Yes, it was," I said.

Markie looked around. "Is he still here?"

He was there all right, standing behind Markie.

Markie sniffed. The smell was awful, like rotting fish. "I think I'm getting a whiff of him."

Dean didn't like that one bit. He walked round, kicked out at Markie and got him right on the shin. Then he sat down on the grass and looked carefully at his pointed shoes. "Hope that kick didn't damage my winkle-pickers."

"What are winkle-pickers?" I asked.

He held up his feet. "That's what they call my shoes. Dead cool, aren't they?"

I thought they looked stupid, but I didn't say that.

Markie was dancing about, holding his shin. "I thought ghosts couldn't touch you?"

"I can," Dean said. "I can kick and punch and nobody can see me. It's great being a ghost."

"I can see you now," I reminded him.

"I know. And that's going to be great, too." He rubbed his hands together. "You're never going to get rid of me, Duncan," said Dean.

Chapter 3
Dead Funny

Markie phoned me that night. "Is he still there?"

"He's still here," I said. In fact Dean was sitting on my bed, stinking to high heaven. "My mum's not happy at all. She says something smells funny."

"Of course I smell funny," Dean said. "I've been dead for about fifty years. What do you expect?"

I ignored him.

I pulled the duvet over my head and spoke quietly into the phone to Markie, "My mum thinks I've got a dead cat in here. And he's making an awful mess."

He was too. He had thrown my games about, pulled everything out of my drawers and scattered it around the room. "Mum's going to kill me when she sees the state of this place."

"I'm coming right over," Markie told me.

He arrived about twenty minutes later. As soon as he stepped into the room, Dean tripped him up and Markie went flying and landed in a pile of my dirty washing.

"Where is he?" shouted Markie. "I'm going to get him this time."

Markie had jumped up and was turning this way and that. So was Dean. One second he was in front of Markie, punching his nose, the next he was behind him, kicking him in the backside.

Dean thought it was dead funny.

"To think I came here with a plan to help him," Markie cried.

"What's your plan?" Dean and I said it at the same time.

"It's a brilliant plan," Markie said.

I knew it would be. Markie is the smartest boy in school. I know, because he told me.

"We're going to help him to rest in peace," Markie said.

"How?" Dean and I asked at the same time.

"Ask Dean if he was murdered, because maybe he wants us to find the murderer and get him put in prison. Then he can rest in peace. That happens in books all the time."

Dean shook his head. "I wasn't murdered."

I told this to Markie.

"Maybe he left something unfinished, then, and he wants us to finish it," Markie suggested. "Did he forget to tell somebody he loved them, or something like that?"

"Stupid idea!" Dean sniggered.

"He says that's a stupid idea," I told Markie.

"I'm only trying to help," Markie said. "How did he die anyway?"

Dean looked thoughtful. "I can't remember exactly. It was a long time ago."

"He can't remember how he died," I said.

Markie could hardly believe it. "As if you'd forget something like that," he said.

Dean was trying to think. "I remember I had this firework, and I was chasing a dog with it. That dog was terrified. I was having such a laugh! That's the last thing I remember."

When I told Markie what Dean had said, Markie went mad! "He deserves to be a ghost," he said. "I don't even know why we're trying to help him."

Dean moved up close to Markie and breathed on him. Markie's face went green.

I thought he was about to pass out. "That ghost stinks," he said.

Dean blew Markie right off the bed. Then he turned to me and said, "You tell your pal, Markie, that I don't want any help. I like being a ghost. It's even better fun now someone can see me."

When I told Markie he stood up. "OK, Duncan, that's it," he said. "No more Mr Nice Guy. We're going to get rid of that ghost."

Dean could hardly stop laughing. "Over my dead body!" he said, and laughed so hard *he* fell off the bed. "Get it? Over my dead body!"

Chapter 4

Help! I'm Stuck with a Ghost!

When I woke up next morning there was Dean, still sitting on my bed, still stinking.

"What *is* that smell, Duncan?" My mum asked me at breakfast. "Is that your feet?"

That made Dean laugh so much he pulled the tablecloth off the table and the plates and cups crashed everywhere.

I got the blame for that too.

"We've got to get this ghost to go," I moaned to Markie when I met him at the school gates.

"He's with you now?" asked Markie.

In answer, Dean tripped him and Markie fell flat on his face in a puddle. There was a shriek of laughter from behind us.

"Look at the cool guy!" It was Sunna, the only girl in the school who didn't fancy Markie. "Not so cool now, are you, Markie?"

Markie frowned at her. If you ask me, Sunna's the one he fancies but of course he'd never admit that. I helped him to his feet. "We've just got to get that ghost to go!" he agreed.

Sunna went off laughing.

"She doesn't like him much, does she?" Dean sounded really pleased about that. His one green eye and his one blue eye had a wicked glint in them. "I could make her like him even less." And with that, he stuck out his winkle-picker and tripped her up. Now she was the one who went face down in a puddle.

She was on her feet in an instant, fuming with anger. She looked right at Markie.

"It wasn't me!" he yelled at her. But she wouldn't believe him. She ran at him and grabbed his school bag, swung him round three times and sent him spinning into the bushes.

Markie had never looked so uncool.

It put him in a really bad mood when we went into class. Everyone had seen what Sunna had done and they were all sniggering. Me and Markie aren't used to that. And it was all Dean's fault.

There he was, squeezed into the seat beside me, grinning like a skeleton.

How nobody could see him I don't know. He looked as solid as you and me. Except for the green glow around him ... and the smell. Everybody was moving away from me and sniffing.

"You smell disgusting," Sunna said in a loud voice.

Mr Barr, our teacher, looked up. He was sniffing too. "Have you got a dead dog in your bag, Duncan?" he asked. Then he chuckled. Mr Barr chuckled a lot – and whenever he did, his wig wobbled.

"Did he say I smelt like a dead dog?" Dean asked.

"You do smell like a dead dog," I reminded him.

It was my bad luck that Mr Barr thought I was talking to him.

"Come here, Duncan!" he said. I came up to his desk with Dean just a step behind me.

"You do smell awful, boy!" Mr Barr said, covering his nose with his hands.

That really annoyed Dean. "I'm going to make him sorry he said that," he muttered.

"Shut up!" I shouted. Dean was getting me into even more trouble.

"What did you say?" Mr Barr's voice rumbled like a volcano about to erupt.

"I didn't mean you, sir," I tried to explain.

Then I watched in horror as Dean reached out and lifted Mr Barr's wig right off his head. I reached out too, to stop him – and of course, what did it look like? It looked as if I was the one who lifted the wig.

Mr Barr was screeching at me, covering his bald head with his hands. The class was going berserk. Dean threw the wig across the room. It hit Markie right in the kisser.

"I might have known. You two are in this together! Now you're both in deep trouble!"

We were marched off to the Head's office with Dean dancing behind us, enjoying every minute of it.

"I love being a ghost!" Dean was yelling.

Markie and I just looked at each other.

"We've got to get that ghost to go!" we said.

Chapter 5
Enter Greg

The Head went on and on at us for half an hour. Dean only made things worse by knocking all the papers off his desk when his back was turned. We got the blame for that. Then he spilt tea all down the Head's shirt. We got the blame for that, too. It wasn't fair.

"Were you this much trouble when you were alive?" Markie asked Dean as we walked home. Too bad Markie was talking to a wall at the time. Dean was standing behind him, making faces.

"Hey, look at the cool guys," Sunna shouted, making sure everyone heard her. "One of them's talking to a wall, the other one keeps talking to himself."

Everybody was laughing at us, and me and Markie. Well, we're just not used to that.

Everyone that is, except Greg. Greg is the school nerd. You know the type – prefers reading books to going to the cinema. And when he goes on the computer, he's finding out stuff for projects, instead of doing something useful, like playing games. He looks just like that Harry Potter – dark floppy hair and glasses. All he needs is the scar.

Greg was studying us now, as if we were a new project. When Sunna and her friends moved off, he walked across to me and Markie. "It seems to me that you and your friend are behaving in a very strange manner," he said.

Greg always talks like that. No wonder he annoys everybody.

"There must be a reason why you two are behaving so oddly," Greg went on. "I ask myself what that reason could be. I hate to admit it, but I haven't got a Scooby. Would you like to tell me what's going on?"

My eyes lit up. I turned to talk to Markie.

"Markie," I said, "this could be the answer to our prayers. Greg is really clever. He knows everything. He could help us ..." Then I mouthed the next few words because

I didn't want Dean to hear, "... he could help us get this ghost to go."

Markie wasn't keen. "He's a nerd, Duncan. It'll spoil our image if we're seen with someone like Greg."

Dean leaned closer to Markie and me. "What are you two whispering about?" he hissed.

Greg leaned closer to us too. Too close. His face turned green as the full force of Dean's stink hit him. "What is that awful smell?" he said.

Dean sniffed under his arms. "It's not me. And I don't like you saying it is." With that, he butted Greg on the nose. Greg fell back and Markie grabbed him just before he fell.

"Who did that?" Greg asked.

"If we tell you, you'll never believe us," I said.

Greg held his nose and looked from Markie to me. "Try me," he said.

So we told him everything. We told him how I had first seen Dean just after my bump on the head, and how he was still there, but only I could see him. We told him Dean wanted to stick around me – for ever.

"It would seem the bump on the head has made it possible for you to see ghosts. Things like that do happen," Greg said, nodding his head very wisely. And holding his bleeding nose. "You say he's dressed in a funny way?"

"Dressed funny!" That annoyed Dean. "Let me tell you, everyone thinks I'm dead cool. I'm a teddy boy."

"He says he's a teddy boy," I told Greg.

Greg's eyes lit up. "Yes, I've heard of them," he said. "They wore tight black trousers and long pointy shoes called winkle-pickers. And they were 'cool' in their day. Myself, I always thought they looked stupid."

Dean's answer to that remark was to punch Greg on the nose again.

"I could help you get rid of him," Greg said, wiping blood from his nose. He looked angry now.

"Do you think so?" Dean snarled and aimed one of his kicks at Greg. He caught him on the ankle.

Greg let out a yelp.

"He's driving us potty, Greg. Now, if you're so clever, how are you going to help us get rid of him?" I was almost begging him.

"You're hurting my feelings, Duncan," Dean said as he took a step closer. "But let me tell you, you'll never get rid of me. You're stuck with me for ever."

Then he grinned, and that's when he was really scary looking. His face went green and his teeth went black.

Stuck with him for ever? The idea made me scream, "Greg! You've got to help us. We've got to get that ghost to go!"

"All right," said Greg. "I'll help you. But on one condition. You've got to do something for me."

Chapter 6

From Worse, to Even Worse!

What Greg wanted was not what we had expected. He didn't want money. He didn't want Markie to get him a girlfriend. All he wanted was to be cool. He told us he was fed up with being a nerd. He wanted to be our friend. One of our gang.

That was the hardest thing to promise. Greg was the kind of guy we tried to stay away from. He wasn't normal – he always did his homework. However, what choice did we have? So, we promised he could be our friend and he promised to help us. He was going to find out all he could to help us get rid of Dean.

Dean was one step behind me all the way home. He kicked a dog (his favourite sport) and it yelped and I got the blame. The owner was Mrs Todd who lived in our street, and she said she was going to phone my mum – so Dean kicked her, too. Mrs Todd lifted me by the ear and dragged me home.

Was my mum mad!

"Kicking Mrs Todd's dog! And then kicking Mrs Todd! I'm ashamed of you, Duncan."

"But Mum," I kept trying to explain. She wouldn't let me say a word. She only sniffed.

"And as for those feet. They stink. Get in a
bath."

The worst thing was that Dean stayed in
the bathroom with me the whole time. He
sat on the toilet, and talked about how
much he enjoyed being a ghost and how he
would never leave me.

I phoned Markie the first chance I had.

"I'm going crazy. I don't care if Greg is a nerd. He can marry my sister if he helps us!"

"This whole thing is so bad for our image, Duncan. Letting Greg be our friend is the worst thing we could do."

"It's OK for you," I said. "You're not the one with the ugly ghost sitting on your bed. You're not the one everybody thinks smells."

I knew that would get through to Markie. He was a true friend. What was happening to me was happening to him.

"OK, pal. I'll phone Greg and see what he's come up with."

I put down the phone. Dean looked angry. "Did you call me ugly?" he said.

"Look in the mirror. You'll see I'm right," I said.

Then I remembered ghosts can't see themselves in the mirror. "You don't have a reflection, do you? Well, take my word for it. You are pot ugly, pal."

Dean was so mad that he pulled out all my drawers, again, and threw all my clothes over the floor. I jumped off the bed and yelled, "Stop that!"

My mum came rushing into the room just as Dean was pushing all the books off the shelf and I was trying to stop him.

"What is wrong with you, Duncan? What's all the shouting about? And look at this mess."

"It wasn't me, Mum," I tried to tell her. But why should she believe me? Who else could it be?

"You've got an invisible friend?" she asked.

He's invisible but no way is he a friend, I wanted to yell back at her.

She put her hand over her nose. "And if that smell hasn't gone by the weekend, I'm taking you to the doctor. Even a *boy's* feet shouldn't smell like that."

I slumped down onto the bed after she left me. Things were going from worse, to even worse.

Dean was sitting in a corner, laughing like someone who was being tickled with a very large feather.

I wasn't laughing at all. I knew then for sure. I'd got to get that ghost to go!

Chapter 7

We've Got to Get that Ghost to Go!

For the first time in my life I was dying to go to school. I didn't sleep a wink because Dean was sitting on my bed the whole night and he never stopped talking.

"Well, I've had nobody to talk to for years. Can you blame me?" he explained.

I pulled the duvet over my head, but even that couldn't keep out the smell. It was like a barrel full of rotting fish, and it was getting worse every day.

"You look terrible, Duncan," Markie said to me when he saw me at school.

I knew I did. I'd had a look in the mirror this morning. White face, black eyes and

my hair standing on end. I looked more like a ghost than Dean did.

Greg came running over to us. "Hi, pals!" he shouted. I could see most of our class watching him. Greg and Markie and me, pals? It didn't seem right somehow.

"Have you come up with anything?" I whispered.

"Anything for what?" Dean whispered too.

When Dean was this close it was hard not to vomit because of the smell.

Greg nodded. "We are going to exorcise him."

"Do you mean exercise him?" I said. "He gets enough exercise following me everywhere."

Greg looked at me as if I was daft. "Not ex-ER-cise. EX-OR-CISE!" He said it very slowly.

Markie and me looked at each other blankly. "Eh?"

"It means ... how to get rid of a ghost."

Now he had our attention. "You know how to do it?" we gasped.

Greg stood proudly. "I went to the library last night and read every book I could about ghosts and why they haunt people. This one just seems to enjoy it."

Dean giggled. "Got that right," he said.

Greg went on talking, "And I read about how to get them to go, too. EX-OR-CISE," he said it again.

Markie jumped on Greg as if he'd just scored a goal. "You're brilliant, Greg!" he shouted.

I jumped on both of them. "What a guy!"

The whole school was looking at us now. But for once, me and Markie didn't care if we didn't look cool. Or if people thought Greg, the nerd, was our friend. We had all been through too much.

Dean just stood there watching us.

"What does he mean?" Dean asked.

It was lucky for us that Dean was the thickest ghost you could ever have come across. He hadn't a clue what we were up to.

He made sure that day was another nightmare for me and for Markie, and now for Greg, too.

He knocked over Greg's class project, a whole jarful of frogs, and they jumped everywhere. It had taken Greg weeks to collect them and he was almost in tears.

Even worse, Dean locked the science teacher in the cupboard with the frogs, and threw away the key. She was in there all day, shouting and screaming, and of course it was Greg who got the blame.

"We've got to get that ghost to go!" he wailed.

In the canteen at lunchtime, Dean shoved Markie's head into his dinner just when he was trying to show Sunna how cool he could be. And it's very difficult to look good with a face full of mashed potatoes.

Sunna went off giggling with all her friends and Markie wailed, "We've got to get that ghost to go!"

In the boys' toilets Dean locked Big Harry, the biggest boy in the school, in one of the cubicles, and guess who got the blame? Yes. Me. I was the only other one there, who else could have done it? And what did I get in return? Big Harry pushed my head down the toilet and flushed.

He said it might get rid of the smell.

The smell was everywhere. By the end of the day I had been put in a corner of the classroom, on my own. Not on my own, of course. Dean was there, right beside me. Grinning.

I had only one thought in my head, *We've got to get that ghost to go!*

Chapter 8
Dead Scared

After school the three of us headed for the park. Greg said it was important to go to the place where Dean had first appeared. That was where he had to disappear, too.

I say the three of us, but it was the four of us actually. Dean was there, following close behind us, every step of the way.

"Where are we going?" he kept asking.

When he saw we were getting near the park he started jumping about wildly. "I love going to the park," he said. "Now, where's that stupid Ross and his stray dogs? I hate those animals. Do you know, my worst nightmare would be to have to live in his house."

Just at that moment, Ross came round a corner, holding six of his dogs on leads. As soon as the dogs saw Dean they began to whine and growl and bark.

"Look!" shouted Dean. "They're dead scared of me! This is great!" And then he was off making faces, getting ready to give those poor dogs another kicking.

The dogs watched him coming. They strained at their leads. They whined. They pulled Ross right off his feet. Then they were off, as if the devil himself was after them. And he was. The devil's name was Dean!

"Come back here!" I shouted. But Dean wasn't listening. He was having too much fun.

"Where is he now?" Greg asked.

"Chasing Ross and his dogs. Look!" It *was* funny. You couldn't help laughing. Ross was being dragged behind the dogs, trying to control them. And Dean gave Ross a few kicks as he ran past him.

"We can't get rid of Dean if he's not here," shouted Greg. "Get him back!"

So we had to wait until they'd all run right round the park and came up close to us again. It was Markie and me who grabbed Ross and stopped him and his dogs from running past us again.

"Do you want your dogs to stop dragging you round this park every day?" I asked.

Ross nodded.

"Well, tie them to a tree and do whatever we do."

We *all* had to work hard to tie up the dogs. They just didn't want to stay. They were going wild.

Dean thought we were trying to help him. "Thanks, boys," he said. "Now I can scare them and they can't even run away."

I felt sorry for the poor dogs. "It won't be for long," I tried to assure them.

"This *is* going to work, isn't it?" Markie asked Greg.

"Of course!" Greg said. Then he added in a voice that didn't sound too sure, "I hope."

He took a deep breath. "Do everything I do," Greg said.

We all took a deep breath.

He started chanting Indian music first.

"I can't understand what he's up to," Markie started to say. Greg told him to shut up and join in. So he did. We all did. Greg's eyes crossed. Our eyes crossed. He started dancing on the spot.

"Is he sick?" Ross asked.

Then Greg started chanting again. This time we could hear the words:

"We've got to get that ghost to go!

We've got to get that ghost to go!"

I joined in:

"We've got to get that ghost to go!"

Suddenly, Markie joined in too. Only he was singing it as if it was a rap song:

"We've got to get that ghost to go!

We've got to get that ghost to go!

We've got to get that ghost,

We've got to get that ghost,

We've got to get that ghost to go!"

Greg wasn't pleased. "This isn't a joke," he said.

But nobody listened to him. I liked the rap, so I started singing it too. So did Ross. Mind you, he had a voice like one of his howling dogs. He sounded awful.

And after a minute or two the beat got to Greg and he started dancing and singing it with the rest of us.

I don't know what we must have looked like. Four boys in the middle of the park singing a rap song and dancing around, with a pack of howling dogs tied to a tree beside us. Lucky we weren't arrested.

Even Dean joined in. He started dancing and singing as well:

"We've got to get that ghost to go!

We've got to get that ghost to go!

We've got to get that ..."

Suddenly, he stopped singing.

"Wait a minute, are you trying to get rid of me?"

Told you he was thick.

But we didn't stop singing, and a worried frown spread across Dean's face.

"I feel funny," he said.

"It's working!" I shouted. "Keep singing!"

I could see Dean was fading, a little at a
time. First his toes, then his ankles, then
right up to his knees.

"Hey! Where's my legs?"

By the time he shouted that, he had disappeared right up to his waist.

He knew he was going and there was nothing he could do to stop it. But when he looked at me he had the most wicked grin you could imagine.

"You won't get rid of me!"

There was only his face left, an angry face. And his voice. A voice that was full of venom.

"You haven't seen the last of me. I'll be back!"

His wail drifted through the air and sent a shiver all through me. The dogs stopped whining right at that moment and their tails started wagging.

"He's gone, hasn't he?" Markie shouted.

"He says he'll be back, and I believe him."

Greg nodded wisely. "Yes, I think he will, too. But not as a ghost. He'll come back as something else, something quite different."

"What?" I asked.

Just then the dogs began barking again and straining at their leads.

"What's wrong with them now?" Markie asked.

At that very moment we noticed the ugliest cat peering through the bushes. A skinny, ginger cat. It arched its back, and bared its teeth and spat at the dogs.

Soft-hearted Ross picked it up. "Aw, the poor little thing," he said, trying to cuddle it.

The "poor little thing" scratched him, and struggled to be free.

A sudden thought came to my head. I looked at Greg. "You don't think it could be ...?"

Greg bent down closer to the cat. "You mean ... Dean?"

The cat spat and sprang at him, claws out. It gripped onto his face and wouldn't let go. It took all of us to pull its claws free from Greg. Then the cat leapt to the ground and was off. When the dogs saw it run, they broke free from their leads and in a flash they were after it.

"If that cat is Dean," I said, "I don't feel at all sorry for it. Dean chased those dogs often enough. They're getting their own back now."

Greg's face was covered in blood. "It's Dean all right," he said. "It's got one green eye and the other one's blue."

Markie jumped in the air. "We did it!" He jumped on me. "We did it, Duncan!"

I jumped on him too and then we both jumped on Greg. "We did it!"

Ross jumped on the lot of us. "We did it!" Then he looked baffled. "What *did* we do?"

Chapter 9
Dead Cool

So, things went back to normal after that. No, not back to normal. In fact, everything changed.

We had to stay friends with Greg. He'd saved us. And we had promised we'd teach him how to be cool. But, you know, when the ginger cat scratched his face it left a great big scar, right on his forehead. So now, he really does look like Harry Potter, scar and all, and let's face it, that makes him pretty cool.

Anyway, being cool isn't so important now. After all, Dean thought he was cool and there is no way me and Markie ever want to be like Dean.

Markie and Sunna are always together now, and somebody has scrawled:

Markie loves Sunna

in the boys' toilets.

I hope it wasn't Markie who wrote it, but I always had a funny feeling he fancied Sunna.

Sunna says she started to like Markie when she saw him with a face full of mashed potatoes.

"But I looked stupid," Markie reminded her.

"I know. But I think I prefer you that way," she said.

Ross has decided he's our friend now too. He waits for us at the park every day, and sometimes even comes with us to the cinema at the weekend. Funny thing is, he's really good fun. I don't know why we didn't let him be our friend before.

He has also adopted the ginger cat. Took it home with him to live with all the other strays. "Well, we've only got dogs," he explained. "I've always wanted a cat."

He's even called the cat Dean. And almost every day I see it being chased by at least one of Ross's dogs.

Dean's worst nightmare has come true. He always said he would hate to live in Ross's house with all those dogs.

And me?

Well, I haven't seen another ghost since then.

Or have I?

Dean looked like flesh and blood. He looked as solid as Markie or me. So, how would I know if I haven't seen a ghost?

How would you?

You could be passing one in the street and not know it.

Or you could be standing with one at the bus stop.

Or sitting beside one at the cinema.

They could be all around us, and we don't even know it.

There could be a ghost sitting beside you right now.

Makes you think, doesn't it?

Barrington Stoke would like to thank all its readers for commenting on the manuscript before publication and in particular:

Duncan Adams
Margaret Addison
Sarah Ali
Mrs S. Barnes
Louise Barrett
Fiona Cameron
Mark Capstick
David Clement
Michael Conner
Graeme Goodwin
Qasim Hanif
Jonathan Hoggarth
Anis Idrees
Iram Iqbal
Namila Iqbal
Rahul Islam
Lee Johnson
James Lafferty

Sean Lafferty
Kirti Liddington
Joe MacDonald
Mrs MacLean
Gary Mitchell
Alexander Mungall
James Murphy
Fiona Newby
Allan Paterson
Gary Rankin
Ross R. Richardson
Scott Ross
Fraser Shaw
Kyrstine Shaw
Grant Stibbles
Ian Swidenbank
Usmaan Waheed
Lauren Whitfield

Become a Consultant!

Would you like to give us feedback on our titles before they are published? Contact us at the email address or website below – we'd love to hear from you!

E-mail: info@barringtonstoke.co.uk
Website: www.barringtonstoke.co.uk

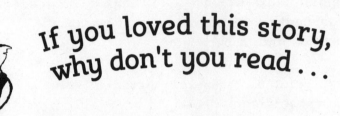

If you loved this story, why don't you read ...

Picking on Percy

by
Catherine MacPhail
Illustrated by Karen Donnelly
ISBN: 1-842990-59-4
£4.50

Has anyone ever picked on you?
Shawn is making Percy's life a misery. But
he is in for a shock when he discovers to
his horror that he is living Percy's life!
Will their lives ever be the same again?

You can order this book directly from
our website:
www.barringtonstoke.co.uk